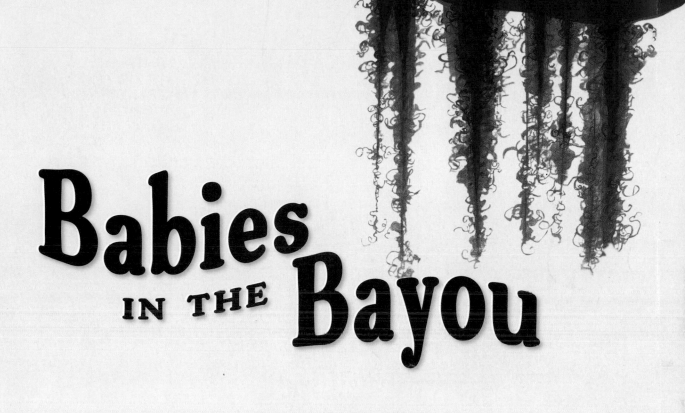

Babies
IN THE Bayou

JIM ARNOSKY

G. P. Putnam's Sons

AUTHOR'S NOTE:

A bayou is a Southern waterway that mixes with the sea.

It can be pronounced bye-you or bye-yo.

G. P. PUTNAM'S SONS
A division of Penguin Young Readers Group
Published by The Penguin Group
Penguin Group (USA) Inc., 375 Hudson Street, New York, NY 10014, U.S.A.
Penguin Group (Canada), 90 Eglinton Avenue East, Suite 700, Toronto, Ontario, Canada M4P 2Y3
(a division of Pearson Penguin Canada Inc.).
Penguin Books Ltd, 80 Strand, London WC2R 0RL, England.
Penguin Ireland, 25 St. Stephen's Green, Dublin 2, Ireland
(a division of Penguin Books Ltd.).
Penguin Group (Australia), 250 Camberwell Road, Camberwell, Victoria 3124, Australia
(a division of Pearson Australia Group Pty Ltd).
Penguin Books India Pvt Ltd, 11 Community Centre, Panchsheel Park, New Delhi - 110 017, India.
Penguin Group (NZ), Cnr Airborne and Rosedale Roads, Albany, Auckland 1310, New Zealand
(a division of Pearson New Zealand Ltd).
Penguin Books (South Africa) (Pty) Ltd, 24 Sturdee Avenue, Rosebank, Johannesburg 2196, South Africa.
Penguin Books Ltd, Registered Offices: 80 Strand, London WC2R 0RL, England.

Published simultaneously in Canada. Manufactured in China by South China Printing Co. Ltd.
Design by Marikka Tamura. Text set in FC Cooper Oldstyle Demi.
The artist used very transparent acrylic colors, adding opaque acrylic paint only for the whites and blacks
on paper, to create the illustrations for this book.
Library of Congress Cataloging-in-Publication Data
Arnosky, Jim. Babies in the bayou / Jim Arnosky. p. cm.
Summary: There are many babies in the bayou, and even though they might have sharp white teeth, hard shells, webbed feet,
or quick claws, their mothers still need to protect them. [1. Bayous—Fiction. 2. Animals—Infancy—Fiction.]
I. Title. PZ7.A384Bab 2007 [E]—dc22 2006011910 ISBN 978-0-399-22653-3
1 3 5 7 9 10 8 6 4 2
FIRST IMPRESSION

For Sarah

In the bayou, where
hanging moss droops
from the trees

and white birds wade
in shallow water,

an alligator floats near her babies,
all sleeping on a log.

There are babies in the bayou
with black and yellow tails

and smiling mouths with rows
of sharp white teeth.

Mother alligator
guards her babies well.

She lets no one come near.

There are babies in the bayou
with rings around their tails.

Each little face is masked in black.

Their mother shows them
how to dig for
tasty turtle eggs.

There are babies in the bayou
with shells upon their backs

and strong little legs to carry them.

One after another the tiny turtles plop into the water.

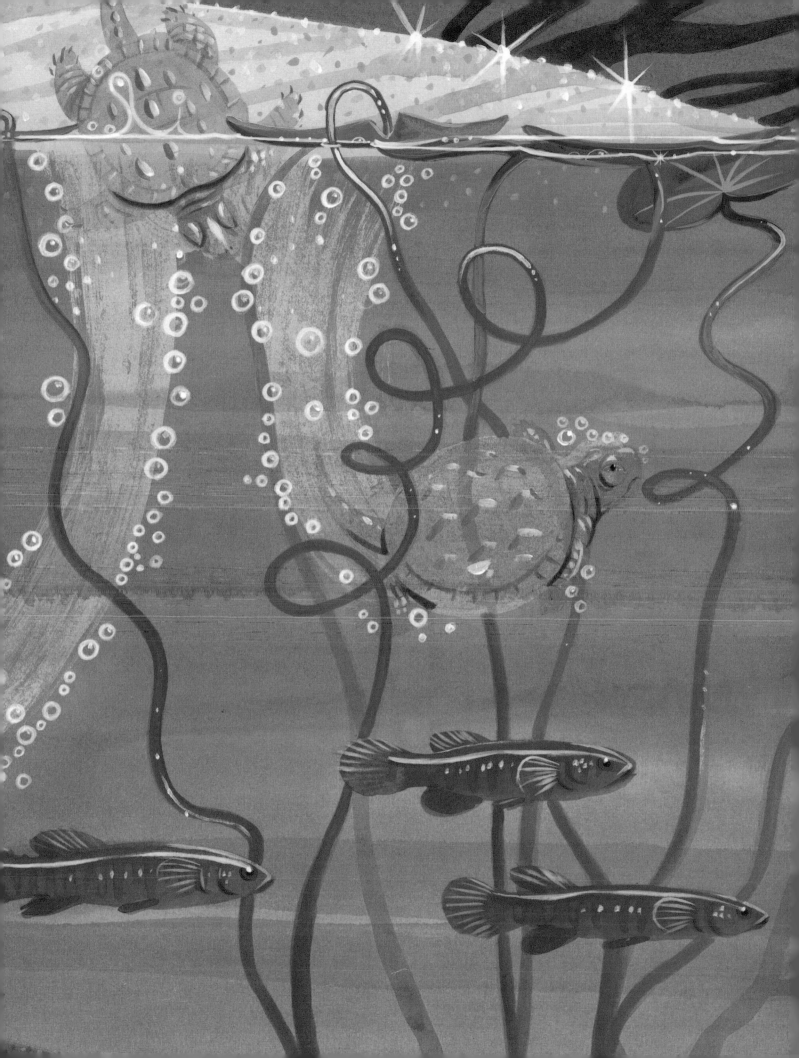

There are babies in the bayou

with webs between their toes.

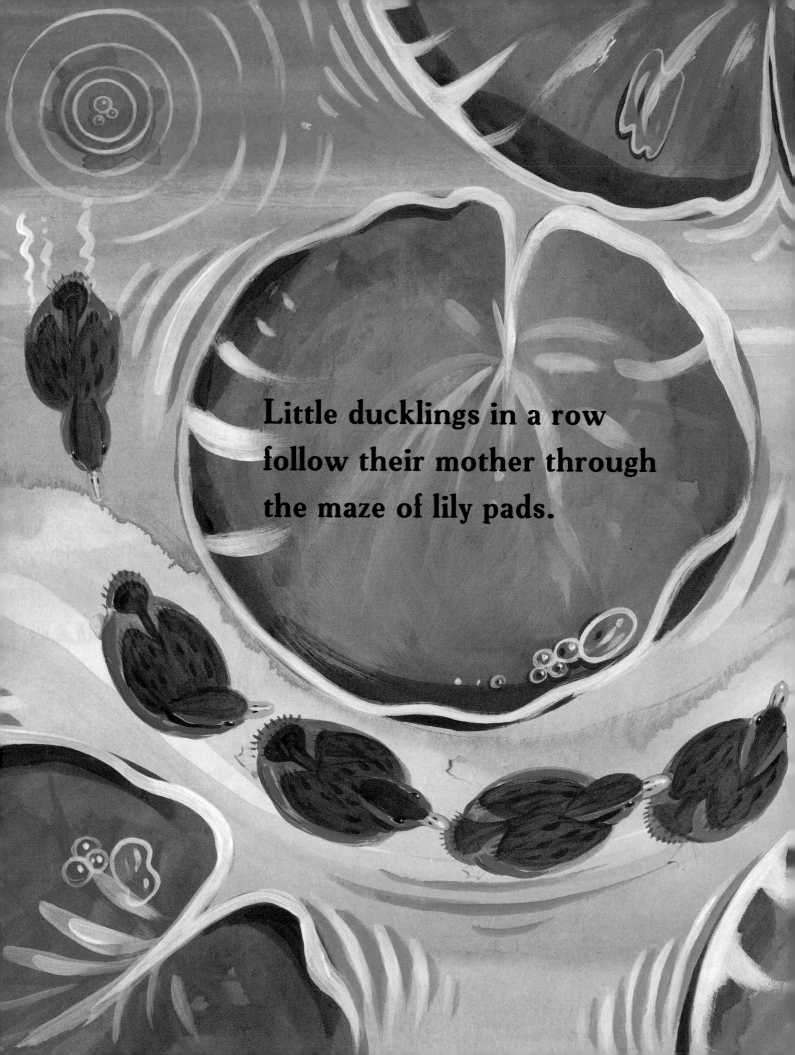

Little ducklings in a row
follow their mother through
the maze of lily pads.

She shepherds them away
from danger—

—away from hungry mouths
with rows of sharp white teeth.

There are babies in the bayou
with black and yellow tails.